CW00545335

EARLY ENGLISH
PORCELAIN

Detail of a Bow figure, *c*.1770. 12in/30.5cm high

Cover Chelsea platter (*detail*), *c*.1765. 12⁵/₈in/31.8cm long

Endpapers *London: The Thames on Lord Mayor's Day* (*detail*)
by Canaletto, 1747

THE DECORATIVE ARTS LIBRARY

EARLY ENGLISH PORCELAIN

By

Bevis Hillier

WALKER BOOKS
LONDON

To Diana Holman-Hunt

Series Editors
Mirabel Cecil and Rosemary Hill

First published 1992 by Walker Books Ltd
87 Vauxhall Walk, London SE11 5HJ

Text © 1992 Bevis Hillier

Printed and bound in Hong Kong by
South China Printing Co. (1988) Ltd

British Library Cataloguing in Publication Data
A catalogue record for this book is
available from the British Library
ISBN 0-7445-1893-8

-Contents-

-Preface-

This book covers the British porcelain factories founded before 1750. So Chelsea, Bow, Derby and Longton Hall are in; but Worcester (founded 1751), Liverpool (*c*.1754–55) and Lowestoft (*c*.1757) will appear in a later volume.

Since my last book on porcelain was published in 1968, excavations and research have revolutionized our knowledge of the early factories; have identified, indeed, factories of whose wares we formerly knew next to nothing – Limehouse, Pomona, Vauxhall, West Pans. The whole subject of British eighteenth-century ceramics is in flux: this book tells the story so far.

Chelsea teapot in the strawberry-leaf style, decorated in Kakiemon palette, *c*.1745–49

B.H.

While the frantic quest for porcelain was continuing in Europe, aristocratic families sent to China to have whole dinner services decorated with their coats of arms. This service in the *famille rose* style was painted in about 1748.

-The Quest for Porcelain-

If you were young and enterprising in the 1840s, in search of adventure and a get-rich-quick scheme, you could have been drawn to photography or railway-building. A century earlier, in the 1740s, it was porcelain-making that seemed to offer the

The sitters' poses in this picture, thought to be by the English artist Richard Collins, demonstrate different ways of holding porcelain tea-bowls, which, like the silver on the table, are indicative of wealth and fashion, c.1725.

best prospects to talented young men prepared to take a gamble. Some succeeded, such as Nicholas Sprimont at the Chelsea factory or Thomas Frye at Bow. Others failed, like Nicholas Crisp of the Limehouse and Bovey Tracey factories. In 1775, a year after Crisp's death, the great Staffordshire potter Josiah Wedgwood – the ceramics success-story of all time – wrote to his own partner, Thomas Bentley: "Poor Crisp haunts my imagination continually – ever pursuing – just upon the point of overtaking –

Admiral Byng caricatured with his collection of china. Byng was shot for cowardice in 1757 and his penchant for porcelain was considered part of his weakness.

but never in possession of his favourite subject!"

There were enormous profits to be made in china manufacture: by the end of the year 1750–51, Bow porcelain sold amounted to nearly £10,000 at a time when a farm labourer's wage was roughly £8 a year; by 1754–55 sales had risen to £18,000. But fortunes were also lost in crackpot schemes. For several of the factories, newspaper reports of proprietors' bankruptcies are part of the sparse documentation that survives.

At the beginning of the eighteenth century, porcelain was a valuable and prized material. Miraculously delicate, milk-white and translucent, it was impervious to fire and water and did not tarnish or rust in the air. Emperors and kings kept it in their treasuries, along with gold, silver and gems. In 1705, having failed as an alchemist to turn lead into gold, Johann Friedrich Böttger was relegated by the Elector Augustus of Saxony to the position of ceramic experimenter. In disgust, Böttger scrawled an angry rhyme above his workroom door.

Gott, unser Schöpfer
hat gemacht aus einem Goldmacher einem Topfer
(God, our creator, has turned a gold-maker into a potter)

Probably the Elector was almost as interested in making porcelain as in finding a cheap source of gold. If so, he must have been delighted by Böttger's progress, which led to the brilliant triumphs of the Meissen (Dresden) porcelain factory.

Porcelain was known as "china" because China was where the best porcelain came from. Aristocratic English families ordered services of Chinese porcelain, decorated in China with their coats of arms. Sometimes the Chinese decorators got it wrong: the Blake family found that on every plate their motto, Think and Thank, had been rendered Stink and Stank. Another English client sent an engraving of his arms, writing in the words blue, red and so on. The Chinese laboriously copied out the words, leaving the arms uncoloured.

What the potters of Europe most wanted to discover was the secret of Chinese hard-paste porcelain, which was made with *petuntse* (china stone) and *kaolin* (china clay) – both degraded forms of granite. At Meissen, the Saxons did succeed in making hard-paste porcelain; but the china made at the St Cloud factory in France, in the late seventeenth and early eighteenth centuries, was in fact a beguiling fake – a soft paste made with a large proportion of powdered glass. The earliest English porcelains, in the 1740s, including Bow, Chelsea and Limehouse, were also soft-paste with a heavy glass content. Later, Bristol, Plymouth and New Hall made hard-paste porcelain.

The race to perfect a porcelain formula accelerated as the fashions for drinking tea, coffee and chocolate took hold. In England, tea-drinking was first made fashionable by Catherine of Braganza, Charles II's queen, and was largely confined to the aristocracy. But tea-drinking was a general practice by the end of the century; and by 1757 Jonas Hanway – in an *Essay on*

Tea, which drew a celebrated riposte from Dr Johnson –
expressed his outrage that beggars and haymakers were drinking tea: "To what a height of folly must a nation be arrived,
when the common people are not satisfied with wholesome
food at home, but must go to the remotest regions to please a
vicious palate!" As the eighteenth century advanced, the tax on
tea imports became a valuable source of revenue for the
government. Early eighteenth-century paintings show upper-
class families drinking tea from handle-less bowls, either Chi-

The London chimpanzee of 1738, engraving by Scotin.
The monkey holds a porcelain tea-bowl.

"The Quarrel with Her New Lover", a scene from *The Harlot's Progress* by William Hogarth (1697–1764). The fashionable tea table is overturned.

nese or in the Chinese manner. In 1739 Thomas Boreman, in a book for young people about curious and uncommon creatures, described a chimpanzee that had been brought to London the previous year and "was very pretty Company at the Tea-table". An engraving by Scotin shows this very human-looking monkey holding a porcelain tea-bowl in its hand. (Monkeys and porcelain – *singeries* and china – went together as trappings of exoticism: Macaulay wrote, of eighteenth-century England, "Even statesmen and generals were not ashamed to be renowned as judges of teapots and dragons; and satirists long continued to repeat that a fine lady valued her mottled green pottery as much as she valued her monkey, and much more than she valued her husband.") Gradually handles were introduced to protect hands from the heat, though some factories were still making old-fashioned tea-bowls in the late eighteenth century.

Coffee was introduced into Italy in 1615 by Venetian traders. By the early eighteenth century almost every shop in the Piazza di San Marco, Venice, was a *caffè*. The first English coffee-house was opened in Oxford in 1650; two years later Pasqua Rosee and his partner, Bowman, established the first London coffee-house in Cornhill. Andrew Duché, the probable founder of the Derby porcelain factory, was a son of a "coffee-man" in Soho, London. Chocolate-drinking also became fashionable in Europe in the seventeenth century.

Something else that favoured the European porcelain industry in its early days was the rapid spread of the rococo style, a style based on curves, shell forms, scrollwork, cartouches, arabesques, as well as interlaced Cs and other calligraphic flourishes, all of which lent themselves to infinitely malleable clay. The rococo brought in asymmetry and femininity, as against the stern symmetry and virility of the baroque which preceded it. Porcelain, especially when decorated, had a feminine charm lacking in beaten metal, carved wood or robust earthenware. By the same token collecting china was sometimes thought to be an effeminate occupation for a man: the china collection of Admiral Byng, who was shot for alleged cowardice, was used to smear him in contemporary satirical prints.

One of the striking traits of eighteenth-century collectors, such as Horace Walpole, son of the Prime Minister, is that they were quite prepared to display new English porcelain wares in their cabinets, alongside Ming and Saxe (Meissen): they acknowledged that something extraordinary was being achieved in their own country, in their own time. Some Chelsea wares now in the Victoria and Albert Museum have the provenance "Strawberry Hill collection" – they were once in Horace Walpole's "Gothick" house at Twickenham, near London.

We do not know which was the first English factory to make a marketable product. Chelsea, Bow and Limehouse were all established in the 1740s and any one of these may have been the first. But the earliest surviving dated pieces are Chelsea jugs of 1745; so this volume, like most on English porcelain, will give Chelsea precedence.

Detail of a Chelsea basket-moulded dish, c.1754. 10⅝in/27cm long

-Chelsea-

In the 1740s Chelsea was becoming a popular riverside suburb of London. It already had three landmarks which it retains today, all dating from Charles II's reign: the King's

Road, the Royal Hospital (built 1682–90 by Sir Christopher Wren) and the Physick Garden, founded on land leased from Sir Hans Sloane.

Sloane (1660–1753) was a doctor and collector. His library and cabinet of curiosities included antiquities, botanical specimens, medals, prints and many other objects collected throughout his long life and various travels. He was the first doctor to

be made an hereditary baronet, and in 1712 he bought the manor of Chelsea and called a street, a square and a place after himself. Today his name survives chiefly in these but to his contemporaries, including the poet Pope, he was best known as one of a small group of fanatical collectors of curiosities. In his "Moral Epistle to the Earl of Burlington" Pope satirizes the kind of dealer who scouted for these eccentrics.

"He buys for Topham, Drawings and Designs,
For Pembroke Statues, dirty Gods, and Coins;
Rare Monkish manuscripts for Hearne alone,
And Books for Mead and Butterflies for Sloane."

Sloane lived to the prodigious age of ninety-three, but died just too soon to see the beautiful use made of "Hans Sloane flowers" as designs on Chelsea porcelain.

On the other side of the Royal Hospital was another of Chelsea's attractions – which has not survived: the Ranelagh Pleasure Gardens. Ranelagh helped to make

Chelsea from the Thames by Canaletto, *c*.1746–48

Chelsea fashionable and created a souvenir market for the china factory. The figures of Ranelagh Masqueraders made by Chelsea in the late gold anchor period (among them Jack in the Green and his partner) are traditionally associated with the masked ball held at Ranelagh in May 1759 to celebrate the birthday of George Frederick, Prince of Wales.

The Chelsea factory was founded, probably in 1744, by Nicholas Sprimont, a 28-year-old Huguenot from Liège. The son of a goldsmith, Sprimont was registered as a London silver-smith in 1741–42. Several pieces of silver by him exist, in flam-boyant rococo style. Much Chelsea china is heavily influenced by silver shapes, and Sprimont continued to make silver for some time after he started making porcelain.

In 1744 he moved into the Chelsea house of Anthony Sup-pley, a Huguenot medical man. Two days later, Sprimont became godfather to Sophie Roubiliac, daughter of the great

The Ranelagh Pleasure Gardens, a contemporary engraving. The masqueraders on the left of the picture are wearing costumes of the kind on which the Chelsea factory based its popular souvenir figures, like the ones on the right. Harlequin and Columbine, c.1760

sculptor Louis-François Roubiliac. For some years a charming Chelsea head of a girl, now in the Ashmolean Museum, Oxford, was known as Sophie Roubiliac (see page 90). This was no doubt wishful thinking; but as Sprimont was on such familiar terms with the sculptor (a fellow Huguenot) at the very time when china production was beginning, it seems likely that he would have asked Roubiliac for help, at the least in lending models to be copied. We know that Chelsea made a delightful copy of Roubiliac's terracotta of William Hogarth's pug-dog, Trump.

Nicholas Sprimont was creative, resourceful and good at public relations: he advertised his wares in fulsome terms from

1744–45 onwards. But one of the reasons he succeeded was that he had rich and powerful backers – among them Sir Everard Fawkener (1684–1758), whose brother William happened to be governor of the Bank of England. Fawkener met Voltaire in France, and he is best known to history for having given the young philosopher a home at Wandsworth, near London, from 1726 to 1729. (Voltaire dedicated his tragedy *Zaïre* to him.) Later Fawkener became ambassador in Constantinople, but muffed the job and was dismissed. He was then appointed secretary to the Duke of Cumberland and accompanied him on his campaigns; Chelsea made a handsome white bust of Cumberland.

Chelsea wares are divided into four main groups, named after the marks used in successive periods: triangle, raised anchor, red anchor and gold anchor. The early pieces, sometimes marked with an incised triangle (note that this is easy to forge), included the Goat and Bee jugs based on a silver original – the British Museum has a rare example marked CHELSEA 1745. The Cumberland bust belongs to this period, as do a bust of a dome-headed baby after the Flemish sculptor François Duquesnoy (Il Fiammingo) and wares with all-over strawberry-leaf (acanthus) and tea-plant patterns. The models of Trump and a white figure of rustic lovers in the British

(*Left*) William Hogarth's pug dog, Trump. 6in/15cm high. Recent research suggests that these dogs were a secret Masonic symbol standing for courage and faithfulness; Hogarth was an active Freemason from at least 1725.

A Goat and Bee jug of about 1745 with the rare incised triangle on its base. 5in/12.7cm high

Teapot decorated by
O'Neale, *c*.1755

(*Right*) Cream jug
showing a scene from
Aesop's fable "The Fox
and the Crane", *c*.1752.
2in/5cm high

Museum are also from this period. Triangle wares have a
high lead content, from crushed glass. The glaze tends to be
cloudy.

The business closed for over a year (from March 1749 to

April 1750) for expansion, and in February 1749 there was a big sale at the factory.

The raised anchor wares which followed (the anchor mark is on a raised pad of clay) are usually thickly potted, the almost opaque glass whitened with lead oxide. The body contains "moons", lighter patches in the greenish-yellow paste, caused by air bubbles. From this period come wares with a moulded scolopendrium-leaf pattern, peach-shaped cream jugs and the characteristic silver-pattern plates, also found with the red anchor mark. Floral patterns and the quail pattern – often used on Bow wares too – were copied from Japanese Kakiemon china. The fine painting of scenes from Aesop's fables, ascribed to Jean Lefebre, William Duvivier and the Irishman Jeffreyes (or Jeffrey) Hamett O'Neale, began in the raised anchor phase. In 1751 the influence of Meissen became dominant; so much so that Sprimont addressed to the government the unsigned *Case of the Undertaker of the Chelsea Manufacture of Porcelain Ware*, urging it to prohibit the import of Meissen. Joseph Willems, a compatriot of Sprimont (born in Brussels 1715), was hired as a figure modeller.

Meissen is still a strong influence in the red anchor period, regarded as the finest phase of Chelsea production. Everard Fawkener got Sprimont access to the collection of Meissen porcelain formed by the English ambassador to Dresden. Many red anchor figures were copies of Meissen originals: for example, the Chelsea Tyrolean Dancers of about 1755 were based on a Meissen group of about five years earlier. Red anchor wares have a luscious, juicy feel to them. The silver-pattern plates often have a thin chocolate-coloured line around their rims. The most sought-after pieces (but to my mind by no means the most appealing) are zoomorphic tureens, moulded as hares and other animals, and vegetable-shaped tureens – melons, bunches of asparagus, and so on. The luxuriant Hans Sloane flower decoration also belongs to the red anchor period.

From the mid-1750s Sprimont suffered from serious illness, and for a time the factory was closed down. In 1756, with the outbreak of the Seven Years War, Meissen exports were cut off.

A pair of Tyrolean dancers (*front and back views*) of about 1755, based on a Meissen original. 6 ⅞ in/17.5cm high

The town was overrun by Prussians, workmen left to find employment elsewhere and Meissen lost its prime place among the china factories of Europe.

The Sèvres factory of France (the royal manufacture which moved from Vincennes in 1756) became correspondingly more important, and the main influence on gold anchor Chelsea. Like Sèvres, gold anchor Chelsea favoured solid-colour grounds of claret and "the inimitable mazarine blue" as Sprimont, who was busy imitating it, called it. Gold anchor sumptuousness is seen at its best in the Mecklenburg-Strelitz service ordered by George III and Queen Charlotte in 1762 as a present for the Queen's brother, Duke Adolphus Frederick IV of Mecklenburg-Strelitz. It is seen at its worst in the later phase, when decoration ran amok – with elaborate piercing, clock-faces set in giant sun-flowers and figures swamped in jungles of *bocage* (greenery). Even the subjects of the figure groups were over the top: the Roman Charity (*c.*1763) shows the aged Cimon, left to starve in prison, being given milk from the breast of his daughter, Pero,

Tureen in
the shape of a
melon (*above*), one of
the most popular
of the Chelsea
designs, *c.*1755.
6¼ in/15.9cm
high

Chelsea
platter (*top left*),
*c.*1765. 12in/30.4cm
diameter

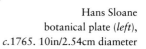

Hans Sloane
botanical plate (*left*),
*c.*1765. 10in/2.54cm diameter

on one of her daily visits. All this on "a pea-green or mazarine blue detachable plinth".

Sir Everard Fawkener died in 1758 – "a man highly unmemorable," Carlyle wrote in his *Frederick the Great*, "were it not for the young Frenchman he was hospitable to." In 1761 a newspaper advertisement referred to Nicholas Sprimont's "indisposition"; his illness was again publicized in 1764. In 1769 the stock was disposed of and the factory was sold to James Cox. Sprimont died in 1771.

Vase and cover (*left*) in Chelsea's famous and highly prized mazarine blue, *c.*1765. 14¼in/36.4cm high

Roman Charity (*above*), a late figure group, *c.*1763. 21in/53.4cm high

-Girl-in-a-Swing Factory-

In 1918 a white-glazed figure of a girl in a swing was presented to the Victoria and Albert Museum. In 1922, William King of the museum staff ascribed this and two comparable figures to the early phase of Chelsea. Like triangle Chelsea, they had a high lead content. They had been made, he thought, under the supposed proprietorship of Charles Gouyn.

More recent thinking is that the figures were made by a different factory in Chelsea set up by some renegade Staffordshire workmen who arrived at the main Chelsea factory in 1747 but soon afterwards defected to set up a rival works in the same area. In 1962 Arthur Lane and R.J. Charleston of the V&A enlarged the Girl-in-a-Swing group to include a large class of miniature scent bottles and other "toys" which had always been thought of as Chelsea.

In newspaper advertisements of 1749 and 1751 we find Nicholas Sprimont crossly dissociating himself from a "Chelsea China Warehouse" in St James's. In 1751 the warehouse proprietor retaliated, stating that his business was not supplied "by any other person than Mr Charles Gouyn, late Proprietor and Chief Manager of the Chelsea-House..." So Gouyn had withdrawn from the parent company and may have joined or backed the seceding Chelsea workmen. It is now believed that Gouyn's factory closed about 1754 and that Sprimont

The famous Girl-in-a-Swing model (*above*), after which the factory is now known.
6½ in/22.5cm high

Finely coloured scent bottle (*left*) in the form of a cockerel from the
Girl-in-a-Swing factory. (*See also page 54.*)

Exceptionally fine Girl-in-a-Swing group, modelled after Raphael's so-called
Small Holy Family

advertised the porcelain "toys" of Girl-in-a-Swing.

Girl-in-a-Swing models – apparently all by the same modeller – tend to be rather prim and expressionless. The modeller
was clearly worried about the fate of the figures in the heat of
the kiln, as he took care to link arms to tree-stumps or other
supports. Arthur Lane, a sensitive critic, conceded that the
unknown modeller's knowledge of anatomy was "rudimen-
tary" but still maintained that, "in 'porcelain-sense', in instinc-
tive understanding of the material, he surpassed all his English
contemporaries." The modeller is seen at his most inspired in
his version of Raphael's so-called Small Holy Family.

In the quest to rediscover the lost history of porcelain, the continuing mystery of Girl-in-the-Swing is perhaps the most tantalizing episode. Only two examples of this model are known; no coloured version has yet been found, but the thought that one may exist haunts the dreams of enthusiasts and the discovery of such a piece is a central, romantic incident in Richard Adams' novel *The Girl in a Swing*.

Leda and the Swan, a Girl-in-a-Swing group, *c.*1749–1754

-Bow-

Of all the young men who took up china-making in the 1740s, Thomas Frye, an engraver of velvety mezzotints and other prints, was the most artistically gifted. His mezzotint self-portrait at fifty is a fine example of his skill. An Irishman, he arrived in London from Dublin about 1734, aged twenty-four. In 1744 he took out a patent with Edward Heylyn, who had been a potter in Bristol and now had a glass business near Bow, Essex. The patent was for "a certain material whereby a ware might be made ... the produce of the Chirokee nation in America, called by the natives UNAKER." Frye and Heylyn may have obtained supplies of the clay through a potter called Andrew Planché, who had baked wares from it in Savannah, Georgia, in the late 1730s.

A period of experiment followed, with financial help from a London alderman, George Arnold. In 1748 Frye took out a second patent, this time in his name only, for making a ware "not inferior to ... China, Japan, or porcelain ware". Words in this patent imply that Frye was now adding calcined bone, or bone ash, to the paste as a strengthening agent – heralding the "bone china" which was England's big contribution to world ceramics.

Just before 1750, Frye acquired two new partners, the London merchants Weatherby and Crowther, and opened a new factory in what is now Stratford High Street (formerly Stratford Road, Bow). In direct challenge to the wares of China, the factory was called New Canton. The earliest dated products of this factory are inkwells inscribed NEW CANTON 1750, which may have been made as promotional souvenirs. The site of the factory was excavated in 1867 for the foundations of Messrs Bell & Black's match factory; some of the Bow fragments found are in the Victoria and Albert Museum. The site was excavated more scientifically in 1921 by Aubrey Toppin, who later became Norroy and Ulster King of Arms. He published his finds in the *Burlington Magazine* of May 1922.

Thomas Frye's mezzotint self-portrait, aged 50, with drawing-board and crayon, 1760. 19¾ x 13¾ in /50.2 x 34.9cm

A lot of the wasters discovered in the two digs were of succulent white sprigged ware in imitation of the Fukien ware of China. One characteristic of the Bow white wares, which include teacups and knife and fork handles, is that where the clay is not covered with glaze, it has tended to turn brown.

Silver-shaped Bow sauceboats with elaborate scroll handles (8in/20.3cm) and a small sugar bowl and cover of succulent white sprigged ware (3in/7.6cm), all *c.*1750

Bow knife and fork handles of pistol form with steel prongs and blades (*right*); the painted decoration includes the Kakiemon style and the Two Quails pattern; 1755–60

Although this could be considered a blemish, it is not in fact unpleasing – the effect is as natural as with a stem on which some leaves are still green while others are turning autumnal.

Bow also made appealing blue-and-white painted wares, the decoration neither mechanical nor haphazard. Painters were engaged in 1753. Some wares were decorated in the Chinese *famille rose* taste, others in Japanese patterns – partridge, hob-in-well, wheat-sheaf, banded hedge and rat. Bow made octagonal plates and bell-shaped mugs with a moulded heart-shaped terminal under the handle. London warehouses were opened in Cornhill in 1753 and in St James's in 1757. Bow must have benefited from the decline in Chelsea's fortunes caused by Nicholas Sprimont's illnesses. It has been claimed that Bow became the

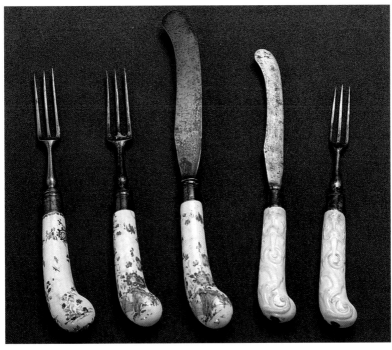

Unusual star-shaped Bow sweetmeat stand of Chinese inspiration with the Koto player pattern (of a zither player beneath a tree), c.1750–60. 5¾ in/14.7cm across

biggest china producer, not just in England, but in Europe.

Bow figures are distinctive. The frontispiece of this book is a fine example. The typical palette used was puce-pink, deepening into crimson; milky blue; pale lemon yellow; brick red and purple. Bow had no modeller as sophisticated as Chelsea's Joseph Willems, whose figures look ascetic and spiritual even when what they are getting up to is not at all spiritual. Figures by Bow's unknown Muses Modeller are slightly vacuous – chinless wonders with neat hair and aquiline noses. When the figures are painted, their noses are like two commas and their parted lips are red. In his book *Bow Porcelain* Frank Hurlbutt included advice on how to sex a Bow figure: "The girl has a smaller, narrower head and a broad plait of hair done up at the back of her head, whereas the boy's hair clings in a cluster of curls all round his head. The Bow girl always hangs her fie-for-shame garment over her left hip whereas the Bow boy as invariably hangs his – shall we say bathing towel? – over his right hip."

Some splendid "documentary" pieces of Bow survive. Housed in the British Museum is the Craft Bowl – a finely potted and decorated bowl in a cardboard box. In the lid of the box is written:

> "This bowl was made at Bow China Manufactory, at Stratford-le-Bow in the County of Essex, about the year 1760 – and painted there by Thomas Craft, my Cypher is in the Bottom; – it is painted in what we used to call the old Japan taste... Miss Nancy Sha, the daughter of the late Sr Patrick Blake, was christened with it. T. Craft 1790."

Octagonal plate decorated with a rare version of the Promenade Chinoise pattern, an Oriental lady taking a leisurely stroll with two boy attendants and a small and excitable dog, c.1760. 6¾ in/17cm

Slightly earlier is the Bowcock Bowl, inscribed JOHN AND ANN BOWCOCK 1759. John Bowcock was on the Bow staff; he was working in the Cornhill warehouse in 1753 and some of his papers are in the British Library. The bowl, which proves that by 1759 Bow had mastered the use of a powder-blue ground, possibly shows Bowcock himself landing from a ship: he had

A parrot eating a nut, c.1760–65

been a sailor before taking work at the factory.

The Bow story, which begins in America with the discovery of the Cherokees' clay, also winds back to America. In 1754 a Boston newspaper announced that Bow china was being imported by Philip Breaking; as no explanation was added, Boston's citizens clearly knew what Bow china was. A 1767 bowl inscribed HALLIFAX-LODGE, NORTH-CAROLINA is in the Museum of Southern Decorative Arts, Winston-Salem, North Carolina; the dated invoice for it survives.

Frye retired from Bow because of ill health in 1759 and died in 1762. Weatherby died in the same year. In 1775–76 the factory closed. Allegedly the moulds were sold to William Duesbury of Derby; but if that is so, it is odd that so few Derby figures seem to have a Bow origin. One theory is that the *coup de grace* to Bow was a new high tax on the American clay. Did the Indian dust bite back?

Bow beaker and trembleuse stand painted in the Kakiemon style with the Two Quails pattern, *c.*1755–60

-Limehouse-

The painting by Canaletto which forms the endpapers of this book shows what the City of London looked like, from the river, on Lord Mayor's Day, 1747. The scene

was dominated, as it still is, by the dome of Wren's St Paul's Cathedral, completed in 1711. If you had sailed downstream and eastwards on the Thames that year, passing the Tower of London, you would have come to Limehouse, where St Anne's Church by Hawksmoor had been completed the year after St Paul's, and where the Limehouse china factory was nearing the end of its brief life.

Limehouse in 1751, an engraving by J. Boydell

John Roque's map of Limehouse in 1746 (detail)

Lion masks from sauceboats, one glazed, the other at biscuit stage, showing moulding

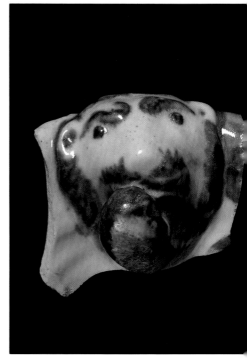

Until 1989, no piece of Limehouse porcelain had been identified. The only evidence that there had been a porcelain factory at Limehouse was a few newspaper advertisements of the 1740s and a couple of other contemporary written accounts. A letter of 1745, sent to William Tams at the Potwork in "Fore Street, nigh Duke Shore" in Limehouse, was quoted in an 1843 book on Stoke-on-Trent by John Ward. An advertisement of September 1746 sought pot-painters to work at the "pot Works at Limehouse". Another advertisement, a month later, gave the name of one of the proprietors: "... Pot, Fan or Box painters, wanting employment, will meet with great encouragement by applying to Mr Wilson, at the Manufactory near Duke-Shore, Limehouse".

By January 1747 Limehouse wares were being advertised; in June a further advertisement offered the public "The new invented Limehouse Ware, consisting of a great variety of useful and ornamental Vessels, which as to Duration, etc., is in no way inferior to China, being now greatly improved..." An advertise-

ment of September 1748 referred to "... Limehouse Ware Tea-Pots, Sauceboats and Potting Pots of various sizes..." Wares were still being produced late in 1747, but soon creditors were invited to meet at the Castle Tavern in Lombard Street; and in May 1748 a final sale of Limehouse wares, including "Sauce-boats, Tea-Pots, etc." was advertised. In July 1750 Dr Richard Pococke, visiting Newcastle-under-Lyme, wrote to his mother "that he had visited a potter there whom I saw at Limehouse".

Joseph Wilson was the potter associated both with the Limehouse and the Newcastle (Pomona) factories. Dr Bernard Watney has recently researched the occupiers of Limehouse in the 1740s and found that Joseph Wilson & Co. occupied a wharf in Fore Street, Duke Shore (Duke's Shore, Duke's Store or Dick's Store), at that time.

By careful measurement, Watney worked out exactly where Wilson's china works had stood; and in 1989 the Museum of London excavated the site. The archaeologists found that all the porcelain was soft-paste. The decoration was of underglaze blue; no other colours. Limehouse wares included simple moulded pickle dishes of either scallop shell or leaf shape, and sauceboats each with three lions' feet supports in turn surmounted by a lion's mask in underglaze blue. Other vessels found on the site included round and octagonal teapots and mustard pots. Also unearthed were fragments of four dog figures from the same mould as a previously known dog figure, which can now be ascribed to Limehouse. "All are white," the archaeologists wrote, "with blue eyes, mouth and toe-nails and appear to be of the whippet variety."

The Limehouse potters seem to have had chronic problems with glazing. The biscuit pieces found on the site were perfectly formed; but with the glazed pieces found, either the glaze is opaque white, dull and bubbly, or the glaze itself is flawless but the body of the ware has buckled.

Fragments including a porcelain dog and tea-bowls

Limehouse studies are still in their infancy. Already some porcelain previously attributed to William Reid of Liverpool has been reclassed as Limehouse. A factory which may have existed from 1744 to 1748 is likely to have produced a large number of wares, even allowing for a high wastage. In time, as more pictures of the Limehouse finds are published, it should be possible to reclaim more wares for this East End factory.

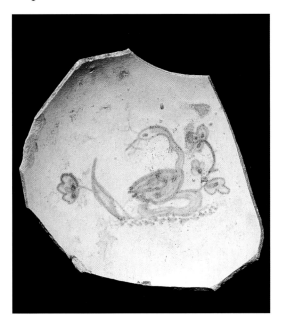

-Pomona-

In 1970 Paul Bemrose of the Newcastle-under-Lyme Museum, Staffordshire, was excavating with his team at Longton Hall when they stumbled on a separate mass of wasters decorated with underglaze blue chinoiseries. One, part of a small bowl, bore the date 25 July 1746.

The finds have been ascribed to the Pomona Pottery. (It takes its name from an inn which later stood on the site: the eighteenth-century potworks was not called that.) In 1747 a Newcastle-under-Lyme potworks was offered for sale. Then owned by William Steers, who in 1744 had taken out a patent for "Transparent Earthen Ware", it was later taken over by Joseph Wilson, formerly of Limehouse. Wilson "seemed to promise to make the best china ware but disagreed with his employers", according to Dr Pococke, writing in 1750 from Newcastle-under-Lyme. Pococke continued: "He has a great quantity made here for the oven, but he cannot bake it with coal, which burns it yellow, wood being the fuel proper for it. I took a piece of what he had perfected there."

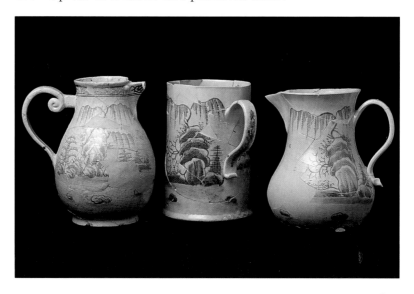

(*Above and left*) Some repaired examples of the blue and white wares discovered on the Pomona site

The soft-paste wares discovered in 1970 included teapots, tankards and spittoons. The main patterns used were peony, a Chinese landscape with a pavilion and big daisyesque flowers moulded in relief and painted blue, which look like the exaggerated blooms in a 1930s Disney cartoon.

There was one tantalizing accident in the 1970 excavation. Paul Bemrose has described how the team found a blue-painted conical cover, apparently identical to those on the "oriental" hats of puff-cheeked child-head tea-caddies formerly attributed to William Reid of Liverpool. "Unfortunately, this specimen was lost when a trench cave-in occurred, completely obliterating its position, and although frantic efforts were made to recover it, the dangerous condition of the trench made a further search inadvisable." This has to rank as the supreme one-that-got-away of English ceramic studies. And at present no one is certain whether Steers or Wilson succeeded in making a marketable porcelain at Pomona or whether the 1970 finds were just a sad cairn of failed experiments.

Some of the finest pieces from the famous Porcelain Room at Fenton House in London, photographed on an 18th-century painted table. At the back, a pair of Harvesters (Chelsea, 12½ in/31.8cm); in front of them a pair of "Dismal Hounds"

(Bow, 3½ in/8.9cm); centre, a black boy holding a dish of fruit (Bow, 6¾ in/17.2cm); at the front on the left, a scent bottle in the form of a cockerel (Girl-in-a Swing Factory, 3½ in/8.9cm); to the right, a Harlequin (Longton Hall, 5¼ in/13.3cm)

-Derby-

The Derby factory was probably founded about 1748 by Andrew Duché from London (not to be confused with Andrew Planché, who may have supplied Bow with American clay). Like Nicholas Sprimont of Chelsea, Duché was a Huguenot and was trained as a silversmith. The two men may have known each other in Soho, where Duché's father sold coffee.

Among early wares attributed to Derby are some very translucent cream jugs dated 1750 with a script *D*. They have a rosy paste and are decorated at the foot with moulded strawberries and leaves. The first contemporary printed mention of the factory is a melancholy one: in 1755 the *Derby Mercury*, reporting that a workman had been drowned, referred to "the China Works near Mary Bridge".

In 1756 a china-making agreement was drawn up between Duché, a merchant banker called John Heath and William Duesbury, of Longton, Staffordshire, "enamellor". Duesbury, who was thirty-one in 1756, had lived at Longton Hall and may have learnt enamelling there. He was in London from 1751 to 1753; his work-books for that period show him undertaking commissions from Derby – for example:

Joun 6 [1753]
2 pr of Dansers
Darby figars 6 – 0

It is perhaps with our hindsight knowledge of Duesbury's later success as a marauding ceramics tycoon that we imagine his arriving at Derby in 1756 as a dynamic new talent. But certainly the paste seems to lighten, the glaze to become chalkier and less

(*Top right*) Mug decorated by Richard Holdship. 8in/20.3cm

(*Bottom right*) Two-handled cup and trembleuse stand, *c.*1758. 6½ in/16.5cm high

Table centrepiece with characteristic marine decoration, *c.*1760–65.
15in/38.1cm high

(*Left*) Figure of "America", *c.*1770. 13¼ in/33.7cm

flawed from that date. Among the useful wares made were sauceboats based on those of Bow, four-lobed globular teapots and tall mugs with handles arching far out from the body. The paintings on mugs and teapots are expansive, using the whole surface as a canvas. Derby knobs on lids are often formed as cherries or strawberries – another quirk copied from Bow. But the transfer-print of a Stag at Lodge seems to be peculiar to Derby. Tiered table centrepieces were encrusted with porcelain shells, corals, crayfish and other slimy things from the deep, heavily daubed with blue.

Unlike the Worcester factory, whose figures are rare, the Derby management seems to have decided early on that figures would be as important a part of its repertoire as useful wares. Derby's ambition was to be recognized as "the second Dresden" – but like the man of whom Oscar Wilde said he had hoped to open a salon but had achieved only a saloon, Derby only managed to be the second Chelsea. The early figures are known as Dry Edge; the lower sides of the base are left bare of the glassy glaze. They include subjects as various as St Thomas, "Chinese Groupe of the Seasons" and Charging Bulls. All these may have been made by Duché before Duesbury arrived at Derby.

The dry-edge figures give a sense of just-suspended movement – they are caught in the act of gesticulating, dancing, shouting, singing, kissing. The later figures are less melodramatic, more reposeful. An early flower decoration used at Derby has been unkindly described as "like a hot cross bun": but by the late 1750s the costumes of figures are often embellished with a more sophisticated "cotton stalk" pattern. Colours tend to be pale, except for a deep yellow and a brick red. In the 1760s, with Chelsea's influence supplanting Meissen's, bases become more rococo, *bocage* is luxuriant and faces are flushed.

In 1770 Duesbury bought up Chelsea and began to use the Chelsea moulds. Today he would be called a corporate raider. According to the great Victorian historian of ceramics, Llewellyn Jewitt, Duesbury not only acquired the Chelsea works; he gobbled up Bow, Limehouse and Vauxhall too.

Four pigeon tureens and covers

-Longton Hall-

In the 1950s a London telephone directory led a researcher to the origins of the Longton Hall porcelain factory two hundred years before. Dr Bernard Watney, a young British Railways accident investigator, knew that a Samuel Firmin had been a partner in the factory. He decided to write to every Firmin in

the telephone book to see if he could trace a descendant.

The first he visited was Jack Firmin, the managing director of an old-established London company of button-makers. In a deed box in Firmin's cellar, Watney discovered two original Longton Hall indentures of 1753 and 1755. The earlier of these referred to a lost agreement of 1751 between William Jenkinson, William Nicklin and William Littler. It stated that Jenkinson had obtained "the Art, Secret or Mystery" of making porcelain.

In 1817 a historian of Staffordshire, William Pitt, told how

Barrel-shaped teapot with painted decoration of the type associated with John Hayfield, known as "the castle painter", c.1755. 8in/20.3cm high

Strawberry-leaf moulded soup plate by the Trembly Rose painter, so called because of his fondness for thin stems and crinkled petals, *c*.1755. 9¼ in/23.5cm

(*Right*) Heron, one of the Snowman figures (4½in/11.4cm)

"about 1750" William Littler, then a salt-glaze earthenware potter, "left Burslem and commenced a porcelain manufactory at Longton, near Stoke." Pitt added that the Longton china, though excellent for its day, had proved unprofitable. In the 1950s, Dr Watney excavated the site of the Longton Hall factory.

He published his findings in *Longton Hall Porcelain* (Faber, 1957). The story he was able to piece together was this. William Jenkinson, a mining engineer, may have done some china-making experiments on his own account. At some time before

1751 he rented Longton Hall, a Queen Anne mansion. In 1751 he went into partnership with Nicklin and Littler.

In 1753 Jenkinson sold his shares to Samuel Firmin, gilder and button merchant. In 1755 a new partner was taken on, the Rev. Robert Charlesworth. Two London sales were held in 1757; a London warehouse was open from 1758 to 1759. In 1760, Charlesworth, foreseeing that he was going to get no return on his investment, dissolved the partnership. In defiance of this action, Littler went on making porcelain for a few months; but his desperate attempt to keep the business going was foiled by Charlesworth's agents. They seized upwards of ninety thousand pieces of porcelain, which were sold at Salisbury in September 1760. Why Salisbury, no one knows; except that the same waterways as brought china-clay to Staffordshire

A pair of putti with a goat, c.1755. 5⅞in/15cm high

from Cornwall could be used in reverse, and Salisbury was a prosperous city.

Early Longton Hall wares probably included the figures known, from their blurred outline under a thick glassy glaze, as Snowmen. A small seated pug dog of this class bears the date 1750. Most of the early domestic pieces bear flower and scroll mouldings after silver originals. A "startling" under-

Leaf-shaped dish with serrated rim and a bouquet painted in the centre over the veins of the leaf, *c*.1755.
10¾in/27.3cm

glaze cobalt blue was used – the celebrated "Littler's blue".

From about 1754 onwards, wares are more translucent and better moulded. Many wares are moulded with leaves, including strawberry leaves and heart-shaped hollyhock leaves. Other English factories used leaf mouldings, but one's first thought on seeing a moulded leaf in eighteenth-century English porcelain should be: Is it Longton Hall?

Wares of the last Longton Hall period, the three years of struggle ending with the Salisbury sale of 1760, included large figures, barrel-shaped teapots, bell-shaped mugs and tall cylindrical mugs with double-scroll handles. Some wares were decorated with transfer prints by John Sadler of Liverpool, including a mug with the arms of Mark Hildersley (1698–1772), Bishop of Sodor and Man, who translated the gospels into the Manx language.

After the factory was so ruthlessly closed down, William Littler set up a china-works at West Pans, near Musselburgh, Scotland. Is it possible that Littler, or one of his patrons, had Jacobite sympathies? A Snowman example of Longton Hall, *c.*1750, is a pro-Young Pretender piece (and in 1750 Charles Edward Stuart was back in London and in the news); and a late mug is decorated with Jacobite symbols. Further, we have Lit-

tler migrating after 1760 to West Pans, not far from Prestonpans, site of the greatest Jacobite victory. Against this theory, Longton Hall made pro-Hanoverian pieces in the Seven Years War and it could be argued that the Jacobite wares may simply have been cannily aimed at an opportunist's market. We can judge how substantial it was from the number of wine glasses that were engraved with Jacobite emblems.

Leaf-moulded bowl (4⅞in/12.5cm wide) and stand (8½in/21.5cm wide) by the Trembly Rose painter, c.1755

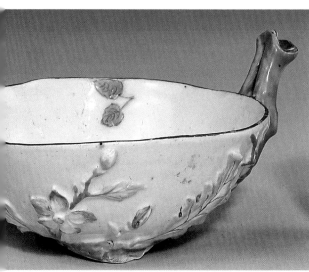

Cylindrical mug (2⅜in/6cm) and peach-shaped bowl for wine-tasting (5½in/14cm wide), c.1755

-Vauxhall-

Nicholas Crisp, a London jeweller and a founder of the (Royal) Society of Arts, was one of those go-ahead men who were attracted to china-making because it

was new and offered the chance of making a fortune. Born in 1704, he was slightly older than Sprimont and Frye. In the early 1740s he and a partner bought a part interest in the ship *Wager*. Between 1747 and 1749, after which it returned to London, the ship was engaged in a trip to Whampoa, near Canton, and may well have brought back a cargo of Chinese porcelain.

By 1742 Crisp had premises in Bow Church Yard. This was

Cream jugs (3in/7.75cm high and 2⅞in/7.25cm high) and vase (5⅞in/15cm high) decorated in underglaze blue, *c.*1755–60

not Stratford-le-Bow, which gave its name to the Bow porcelain factory (the place mentioned by Chaucer in deriding the Prioress's educational pretensions – "And Frenssh she spak ful faire and fetisly / After the scole of Stratford atte Bowe..."); it was the Bow Church of Bow Lane, City of London, within the sound of whose bells every true cockney must be born.

In June 1751 Crisp and John Sanders, a potter from Lambeth, south London, were granted a soaprock licence for a term of ten years. In September, Sanders insured a kiln for £200. The first shipment of soaprock arrived in 1752. In May 1753 a London newspaper advertised "Porcelain in Imitation of the Ware of China". In May 1755 one Samuel Martin paid Crisp a guinea for "four small figures of Vauxhall China". A month later, John Bacon, trainee sculptor and future Royal Academician, was apprenticed to Crisp and modelled figures for him of the shepherd/shepherdess type. Rupert Gunnis, the expert on English sculpture, thought that Bacon's training with Crisp affected his later style of sculpting draperies in a liquid, porcellaneous manner.

In later years, Bacon remembered the factory as sizeable – "at least four storeys high, with three trap doors for the purpose of lowering packages from the upper storeys. The factory had an outer yard closed with 'great gates'." Bacon also recalled how one of the modellers was caught and punished for stealing duplicate moulds for "small figures and other ornamental models of a delicate nature". The early days of china-making in England were a profitable time for industrial spies.

The factory lasted over ten years. Crisp went bankrupt in 1763 and a final sale of Vauxhall porcelain was held in the following year – "curious Figures, all Sorts of ornamental Toys, Knife-Handles ... etc." At about that time Crisp moved to Bovey Tracey, near Exeter, Devon. He set up another china factory, but this too failed. "Poor Crisp is quite a ground," the Plymouth potter William Cookworthy wrote to Thomas Pitt in December 1767. Crisp died at Bovey Tracey in 1774 and is buried there. Visiting the Devon town in the following year, Josiah Wedgwood noted: "A Mr Crisp from London endeavoured to make

Detail of lidded vase on pages 70-71

a kind of porcelain here, but did little more than make some experiments and those unsuccessful ones." If this story of help-lessness is accurate, the limited success Crisp had at Vauxhall may have owed a lot to the practical skills of his partner, Sanders – who continued at Vauxhall, as a maker of plain and blue and white earthenware, after Crisp left.

In the 1980s, the Museum of London decided to excavate the site of a Pothouse, recorded on a survey map as midway between Lambeth and Vauxhall Bridges – on the present Albert Embankment. In 1746 Sanders alone may have been running the pot-works; but certainly this place was where he and Crisp made the Vauxhall porcelain. The fragments unearthed caused a great many wares previously thought to be by William Ball of Liverpool to be reascribed to Vauxhall.

The finest Vauxhall wares are of a surprisingly white paste either painted or transfer-printed with polychrome flowers – fine compositions of blowsy roses and other blooms, well spaced out on the body of the ware. The effect is almost of decalcomania transfers on Victorian vases filled with Shanklin white sand. An Imari palette similar to that of Bow during the same period was also favoured – underglaze blue with touches of overglaze iron red and gold.

Like Chelsea with its Ranelagh Gardens, Vauxhall had on its doorstep a ready market for souvenir wares, in the equally popular Vauxhall Gardens. One Vauxhall bowl is inscribed with words and music from *The Beggar's Opera* "set by Mr Yates" – who wrote songs for Vauxhall Gardens in the mid-eighteenth century.

A rare globular bottle (*right*) painted with Chinoiserie scenes, *c*.1755. 7⅛in/18cm and 6¾/17.2cm high

-Lund's Bristol-

In about 1748 a copper merchant and brassfounder named Benjamin Lund opened a china factory in an old glass-house in Bristol. The soft-paste wares he made are now usually called Lund's Bristol; they used to be called Lowdin's or Lowris's Bristol, after the name of the former glass-house. Some of the wares are marked in relief Bristol or Bristoll and a few figures of Chinamen bear the date 1750.

In March 1749 Lund was granted a licence to mine soaprock in Cornwall. The soaprock made his wares more resistant to heat; some of the London porcelains cracked when hot water was poured on them.

Lund may well have employed workmen from the recently closed-down Limehouse factory, and most of his known wares are of the underglaze blue chinoiserie kind made by Limehouse. Lund's glaze tends to have a bluish tone, because the cobalt blue he used "flew" in the kiln.

In 1751 Lund sold out his business to a consortium of Worcester businessmen. The principal shareholders included Dr John Wall, a fellow of Merton College, Oxford, and a Worcester physician; Richard Holdship, a rich glover; and Edward Cave, editor of the *Gentleman's Magazine*.

In May 1751 Holdship leased Warmstry House, a Tudor mansion on the banks of the Severn. In February 1752 Holdship bought Lund's factory on behalf of the Worcester partners. In August the *Gentleman's Magazine* published an engraving showing the Worcester factory's layout, with its convenient river inlet for soaprock and coal going in and wares going out. From excavations on the Warmstry House site (now the car park of the Worcester Technical College) it is clear that early Worcester wares were virtually identical to those of Lund's Bristol in paste, shape and decoration. In particular, the same double-handled sauceboats were made at both factories, with underglaze blue patterns. It was as if the Lund's factory had

A sauceboat in *blanc de Chine* showing the "Bristoll" mark and a Wigornia type creamboat in underglaze blue with an embossed "Bristol" mark

been magic-carpeted to Worcester. It just is not possible to tell Lund's and the earliest Worcester apart. I would like to propose a new name for these wares: Bricester.

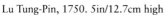
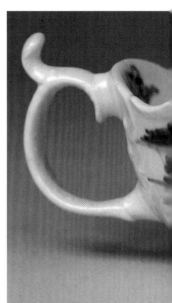
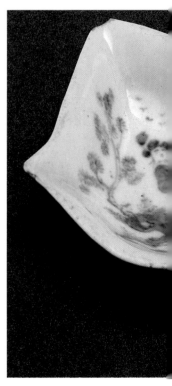

Lu Tung-Pin, 1750. 5in/12.7cm high

(*Top right*) Sauceboat painted in underglaze blue by the "three-dot" painter. 3in/7.6cm high

(*Bottom right*) Pair of leaf-shaped pickle dishes; the decoration shows a sage in a garden. 3⅞in/10.2cm

-78-

-Factory Marks-

Bow	Bow	Bow	Chelsea *1745–50*	Chelsea *c.1750*

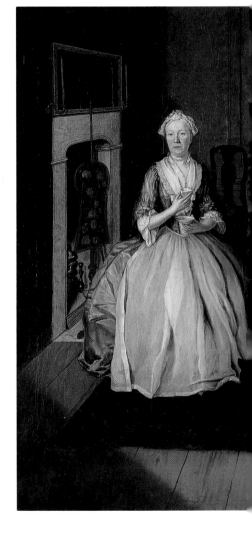

An English family at tea, painted
*c.*1740. Clearly less wealthy than the
sitters in the portrait on page twelve,
they are more modest followers of the
fashion for porcelain.

Chelsea
Raised, 1750-52
Red, 1752-56
Gold, 1756 onwards

Derby
Introduced c.1784

Derby
c.1795

Longton Hall

-Further Reading-

Bow Porcelain, Elizabeth Adams and David Redstone, Faber, London, 1981.

Bow Porcelain – the Collection Formed by Geoffrey Freeman, Anton Gabszewicz, Lund Humphries, London, 1982.

Ceramics of Derbyshire, 1750-1975, H. Gilbert Bradley, privately printed, London, 1978.

Chelsea Porcelain, Elizabeth Adams, Barrie & Jenkins, London, 1987.

Derby Porcelain, F. Brayshaw Gilhespy, MacGibbon Kee, London, 1961.

Derby Porcelain, John Twitchett, Barrie & Jenkins, London, 1980.

Derby Porcelain: The Golden Years 1750-1770, Dennis G. Rice, David & Charles, Newton Abbot and London, 1983.

Derby Porcelain 1750-1798, Gilbert Bradley, Thomas Heneage, London, 1990.

Encyclopaedia of British Porcelain Manufacturers, Geoffrey Godden, Barrie & Jenkins, London, 1988.

English Blue and White Porcelain of the Eighteenth Century, Bernard Watney, Faber, London, 1963.

English Porcelain Figures of the Eighteenth Century,
Arthur Lane, Faber, London, 1963.

The Illustrated Guide to Worcester Porcelain, Henry Sandon,
Barrie & Jenkins, London, 1969.

"Limehouse in the Limelight", Bernard Watney, *Antique
Collecting*, September 1983.

"Limehouse Uncovered", Lawrence Pontin and Julia
St John Aubin, *Sotheby's Preview*, September/October 1990.

Longton Hall Porcelain, Bernard Watney,
Faber, London, 1957.

Lowestoft Porcelain, Geoffrey Godden, Antique Collectors'
Club, Woodbridge, Suffolk, 1985.

Sotheby's Concise Encyclopedia of Porcelain,
David Battie (ed.), Sotheby's, London, 1990.

Staffordshire Porcelain, Geoffrey Godden (ed.),
Granada, London, 1983.

Transactions of the English Ceramic Circle, Paul Bemrose,
"The Pomona Potworks, Newcastle, Staffordshire",
vol. 9, part i, 1973.

Worcester Porcelain and Lund's Bristol, Franklin A. Barrett,
Faber, London, 1966 ed.

-Places to Visit-

Great Britain

Brighton Museum and Art Gallery
Church Street
Brighton
East Sussex
BN1 1UE

British Museum
Great Russell Street
London
WC1B 3DG

National Museum of Wales
(Amgueddfa Genedlaethol Cymru)
Cathays Park
Cardiff
South Glamorgan
CF1 3NP

Cecil Higgins Art Gallery
Castle Close
Bedford
Bedfordshire
MK40 3NY

Fenton House
Windmill Hill
Hampstead
London
NW3 6RT

Fitzwilliam Museum
Trumpington Street
Cambridge
Cambridgeshire
CB2 1RB

Greys Court
Henley-on-Thames
Oxfordshire
RG9 4PG

Holbourne of Menstrie Museum
Great Pulteney Street
Bath
Avon
BA2 4DB

Merseyside County Museum
William Brown Street
Liverpool
Merseyside
L3 8EN

National Museum of
Antiquities of Scotland
Queen Street
Edinburgh
Lothian
EH2 1JD

City Museum and Art Gallery
Bethesda Street
Hanley
Stoke-on-Trent
Staffordshire
ST1 4HS

Upton House
Nr Banbury
Oxfordshire
OX15 6HT

United States of America

Victoria and Albert Museum
Cromwell Road
South Kensington
London
SW7 2RL

Wallington Hall
Cambo
Nr Morpeth
Northumberland

Museum of Fine Arts
465 Huntington Avenue
Boston
Massachusetts 02115
USA

Colonial Williamsburg
Goodwin Building
Williamsburg
Virginia 23185
USA

High Museum of Art
1280 Peachtree Street N.E.
Atlanta
Georgia 30309
USA

Metropolitan Museum of Art
5th Avenue at 82nd Street
New York
New York 10028
USA

Seattle Art Museum
Volunteer Park
Seattle
Washington 98112
USA

Bow figure of a shepherdess, *c.* 1765

-Acknowledgements-

The editors would like to thank the following
for their help in producing porcelain to be
photographed for this book:
Tessa Aldridge of the Ceramics department,
Sotheby's, London
Simon Spero, Kensington Church Street, London
Rotraut Weinberg of the
Antique Porcelain Company,
London and New York

A Bow vase of swollen panel form decorated in a Kakiemon palette, *c.*1755

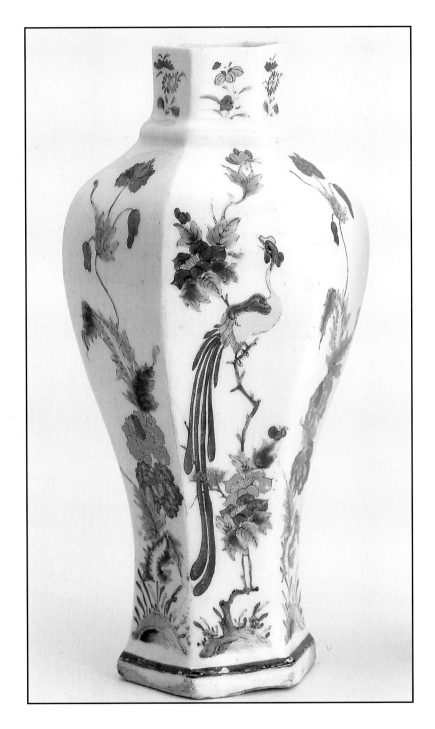

-About the Author-

Bevis Hillier, formerly editor of *The Connoisseur* and of *The Times Saturday Review*, is editor of Sotheby's *Preview* magazine. His first book, published in 1965, was a pioneering study of a Staffordshire potting family of the eighteenth and early nineteenth centuries, the Turners of Lane End. In 1968 he published the acclaimed *Pottery and Porcelain, 1700-1914*. Hillier also set the guidelines for the study of Art Deco with the first English book on that subject (1968). The late Sir John Betjeman authorized Hillier to write his biography, the first volume of which, *Young Betjeman*, appeared in 1988.

The Music Lesson, Chelsea soft-paste porcelain, *c*.1765

-Picture Credits-

Our thanks are due to:

The Antique Porcelain Company, New York: pp.10, 30

The Antique Porcelain Company, London: pp.23, 28, 29

The Ashmolean Museum, Oxford: p.80

Bearsted Collection, Upton House: p.89

Blickling Hall: p.44

Bonhams, London: pp.37, 89

Borough Museum, Newcastle-under-Lyme, Staffordshire/Gerald Wells: pp.52, 53

Bridgeman Art Library: pp.57, 59, 86

Private Collection. By Courtesy of the Trustees of the British Museum: pp.25, 33

Christie's, London: pp.11, 31, 36, 64, 65, 68–9, 82–3

County Museum, Truro: p.58

The Trustees of the Dyson Perrins Museum, Worcester: pp.77 – foot, 78, 78–9

Fenton House/Angelo Hornak: p.21

Gubbay Collection, Clandon Park: pp.60–1, 92

Hanley Museum and Art Gallery: p.26

Bevis Hillier: pp.17, 22, 23

Christopher Lennox-Boyd: p.39

Museum of London: p.26

The National Trust Photographic Library: Frontispiece; pp.34, 54–5

Sotheby's, London: pp.16, 40–1, 41, 42, 43, 44–5, 46–7, 48, 48–9, 50, 67, 75, 78–9

Simon Spero: pp.19, 70–1, 73

Courtesy of the Board of Trustees of the Victoria and Albert Museum: Cover; pp.12, 13, 30, 32, 35, 62–3, 66

Wallington Hall: p.91

Chelsea head of a young girl, formerly known as Sophie Roubilac, c.1752. 7⁷⁄₁₆in/19cm high

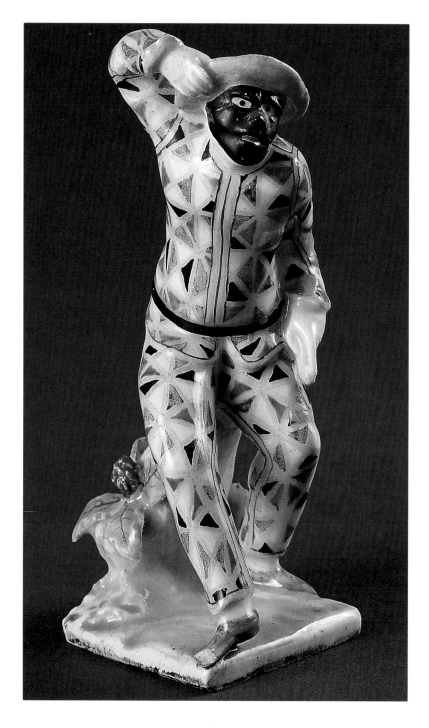

-The Decorative Arts Library-

Early English Porcelain
Bevis Hillier

Modern Block Printed Textiles
Alan Powers

Point Engraving on Glass
Laurence Whistler

Rag Rugs of England and America
Emma Tennant

Bow figure of Harlequin, *c.*1750–55